# *The Book of* INTENTS

INTENTIONS AND AFFIRMATIONS TO INSPIRE

SHILPI JAYESH CHAWLA

# EMBASSY BOOKS
www.embassybooks.in

**Published by:**

**EMBASSY BOOK DISTRIBUTORS**
120, Great Western Building,
Maharashtra Chamber of Commerce Lane,
Fort, Mumbai-400 023, (India)
Tel : (+91-22) 22819546 / 32967415
Email : info@embassybooks.in
Website: www.embassybooks.in


ISBN :  978-93-83359-39-4

*This work is complete with*

*the unconditional love*

*&*

*support of my husband*

*– Thank You!*

*This book is dedicated to me!*

- intent to focus

- intent to be calm and composed

- intent to suspend and release

- intent to connect

- intent to stand in grace and be guiltless

- intent to relax and enjoy inspired action

- intent to acknowledge

- intent to respect

- intent to be visible

- intent to proudly inherit my kingdom

- intent to serve and share

- intent to recognize myself as more than the person in this body

- intent to be strong

- End note

# Introduction

An intent is to clearly state what you desire from the universe.

It is to specify what you would like, be certain about it without a shred of doubt, and then watch it manifest in your life.

Intents seem simple to make, and yet work only in conjunction with a genuine commitment to who you really are.

Even seemingly impossible tasks can be accomplished when backed by the power of an intent.

An intent is your determinism as an individual in action. It is a reflection of your ability to achieve anything in this universe because in truth, you are bigger, better, more powerful and more able than you often believe.

Your ability to create a future from your choosing, makes you cause over the world around you, rather than an effect.

Intentions bring you closest to the creator and reflect the grace of creation in action.

Each of us is uniquely crafted. Your desires may differ from mine, but the techniques of bringing them to fruition are universal. While reading the intents in this book you will probably discover many of your own dormant aspirations, which you may not have confronted or acknowledged.

May this simple book of intents present you with the inner will and gratitude to draw your own intents.

love

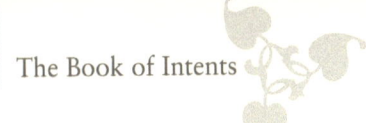

# *intent to love*

*It is my intent to love.*

*It is my intent to hold a loving space that originates from the cosmos into my heart and radiates out to every object of my attention.*

*It is my intent to love unconditionally.*

*It is my intent to release all the buts, ifs, whys, what's, how's and just love for the sake of love.*

*I am in love with life.*

*I attract love in all my interactions and experiences.*

*It is my intent to breathe in and breathe out love.*

*It is my intent to allow love to flow through every part of my body and let the universe nurture my being.*

*It is my intent to be happy and share that with the world.*

tuned
in

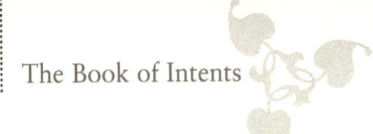

# intent to be tuned in

*It is my intent to be tuned in to the universe.*

*I will revive and refresh myself and care for this body.*

*It is my intent to align with who I am.*

*I allow things to fall into place.*

tuned

in

*I have a constant flow of positive thoughts.*

*My focus and attention is on joy, play and happiness.*

*I am full of appreciation and gratitude for everything I have.*

*It is my intent to be in the universal frequency of ease, accuracy and joyous blissful thoughts.*

*It is my intent to match what I really want from my*

tuned in

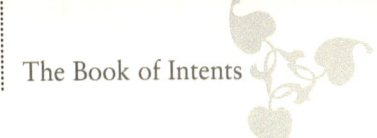

life experience through my thoughts.

I am the master of my thoughts. Each thought having a positive influence on my body and my mind.

I feel the pulse of the universe and I am synchronized with the universal flow.

I enjoy life. With everything I do I am creating joy for myself and others.

Secure

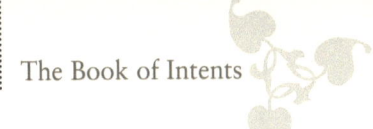

# *intent to be Secure*

*I am secure.*

*It is my intent to know myself as a secure being.*

*I am not afraid to make mistakes because I am secure in my self-worth.*

*I am secure enough to see the good in others and encourage them to find more goodness in themselves.*

13

Secure

*I am open to new experiences.*

*I trust my connection with the source.*

*I am willing to accept myself, exactly as I am.*

*I am undisturbed by what other people may think about me.*

*I am comfortable in my own skin.*

*I am beautifully me.*

Secure

*I am attentive to myself.*

*Each day, I allow life to celebrate who I am.*

*I acknowledge the love that the universe showers on me and others.*

*I forgive that which does not sit with me and return to my own resonance.*

*I appreciate every person I meet, for being unique and expressing who they are.*

# intent to be pure

It is my intent to be *pure*.

There is purity in my thoughts and my way of being.

Pure is powerful, pure is peaceful, pure is authentic. I am pure.

I am genuine and lovingly detached, free from the stress of outcomes.

*It is my intent to allow the energy that creates worlds to breathe through me.*

*It is my intent to feel as pure as God.*

*I trust myself to be the perfect being that god created.*

# appreciate

# intent to appreciate

It is my intent to *appreciate.*

I lovingly appreciate every moment.

I appreciate the small and big details in all that I see.

I am in constant harmony with appreciation.

I choose to be genuine as I appreciate my way through the day.

appreciate

*It is my intent to appreciate and acknowledge every emotion inside of me such that I honour it, embrace it and appreciate myself for willing to do so.*

*It is my intent to appreciate all that I can see and all that may not be visible at the time.*

*I appreciate this planet.*

*I connect with the lives I touch and I appreciate the goodness they have to offer.*

# intent to be in power

I am powerful.

It is my intent to feel the goodness, grandness and glory of my power.

I am connected with the power in my being.

I am present – here and now.

It is my intent to show up to every wonderful invitation that has my goodness written all over it.

*I revel in my power.*

*It is my intent to connect with the unlimited domain of power and feel its alignment, its vastness, its magnificence and be one with it.*

*It is my intent to use my power to ride many waves of Inspiration, Teaching, Learning, Being, and Doing. I enjoy life every moment wherever in the world I may be.*

Victorious

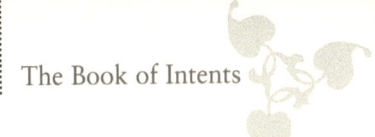

# *intent to be victorious*

I *am victorious.*

I *wake up to each day, knowing, feeling and vibrating win-win victory drumbeats.*

I *am rewarding myself unconditionally.*

I *am talking, walking and writing as a winner. I have the attitude of a winner.*

# Victorious

*There is no doubt in my universe to contradict that.*

*It is my intent to be at ease with the high vibrations and have a high life condition.*

*All around me I can see visuals that support my victory attitude.*

*I look into the mirror and see a person who is creating her dreams and living in sync with her aspirations.*

# belief Systems

# intent to align with new belief systems

It is my intent to instill, be aware and live *new belief systems* that are in alignment with my inner wisdom.

I believe that life loves me immensely.

Life loves me and holds good things in store for me.

Life loves me and backs me up at every instant.

# belief Systems

*The whole universe is working towards my well-being. There is no way I can fail.*

*Life is delighted to serve me in every possible way.*

*I believe that I am open to new and creative ways that are always working out for me.*

*I believe I have something to express and share with the world.*

# intent to download the divine design

It is my intent to download the divine-design of my life.

It is my intent to trust that pattern and its revelation.

It is my intent to manifest the divine-design into my life.

It is my intent to embrace and allow the gold nugget within me, i.e. my consciousness of

divine
design

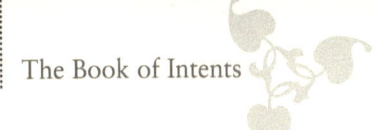

gold, of opulence, to bring riches into my life.

I give praise and gratitude for all the good things that god has granted me in this life.

With every breath, I breathe in love, happiness, abundance and self-expression.

It is my intent to bring my heaven upon earth through right thinking.

It is my intent to practice the Truth that sets me free.

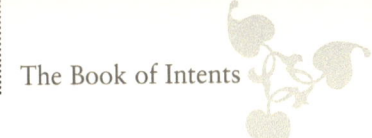

# intent to trust

*It is my intent to trust.*

*I trust the process of life.*

*I flow with life and feel safe within, no matter what happens on the outside.*

*I trust my power of imagination, and believe in my visualizations.*

*I trust my instinct and my intuition.*

*I trust who I am.*

*I trust that the best comes to me, as I venture into different territories.*

*It is my intent to be supported and surrounded by trust-worthy people.*

*It is my intent to be trusted, to radiate trust, to have trust, to allow trust.*

*I trust life to give me what is best for me each day.*

# *intent to be at peace*

*It is my intent to be at peace.*

*I am at peace with the here and now, and that peace radiates through me to my surroundings.*

*My sense of peace is inspiring to those around me such that they are drawn to find their own peace.*

*I am lovingly detached to being at peace.*

peace

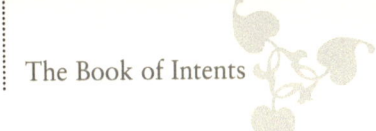

*The present moment holds all the answers and points towards the solutions with such peace.*

*My sense of peace brings balance and opens doorways for compassion and grace.*

*I can sense the source of this peace, and can observe it getting disturbed when I act unlike myself therefore I stay true to who I am.*

*It is my intent to be at ease with my peace of mind.*

authentic

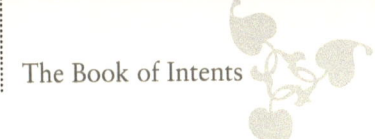

# *intent to be authentic*

I am authentic as I am integrated with the truth of who I am.

I am genuine in everything I do.

I breathe genuinely.

In all situations I am authentic and I sense this truth.

It is my intent to wake up

authentic

*and wake up for good.*

*I am convinced about the awesomeness inside me so strongly that I don't care about opinions.*

*My interest in myself is authentic.*

*I genuinely flourish.*

*accept*

# *intent to accept*

*I accept.*

*It is my intent to accept all of who I am.*

*As I accept to be visible with all that is within, I understand my lows and learn to fly high even with them.*

*I go easy on myself.*

*I understand that my success is inevitable.*

Accept

*I dance through the journey
and revel in it.*

*I accept all opportunities for
me to blossom and bloom.*

free

# intent to be free

I *am free.*

I *free my mind of all limitations.*

It *is my intent to live responsibly with freedom.*

I *walk in free zones, attract free thinking people and nurture their freedom.*

I *clear all clutter and thereby create space for more freedom.*

free

*I free my mind of all conventional ways of doing things.*

*I always act out of the freedom I feel within me.*

*I allow people the freedom to be who they are.*

Compassionate
and kind

# intent to be compassionate and kind

*I am compassionate and kind.*

*I awaken the flame of compassion deep within me.*

*It is my intent to be kind to my mind and heart.*

*I allow myself the necessity to indulge, to be brave, to walk the path less traveled and to comfort my soul.*

# Compassionate
# and Kind

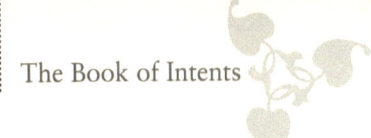

*With my compassion, I bridge the gap between me and others.*

*Each morning, I welcome myself with a warm embrace of kindness and compassion.*

*My gentle nature is felt by all those who cross my path.*

bless

# intent to bless

I bless.

As I feel the power of love, I embrace and bless.

I bless to begin an inner journey of love that is central to my existence.

It is my intent to bless because it feels good.

I give and receive multiple blessings; as many as the heartbeats in my body.

bless

*I acknowledge and receive
with gratitude all the
blessings that come my way.*

*I truly magnify the goodness
of blessings such that it is my
natural way of being.*

believe
in Myself

# intent to believe in myself

*I believe in myself.*

*It is my intent to stay alive to my creation.*

*I remember and recall the love, power and abundance that are part of my natural inheritance.*

*I believe in my own innate power.*

believe
in myself

*I believe that God is my supply and source.*

*I believe that for every demand I have, there is surplus supply.*

*It is my intent to know that those who surround me are inevitably benefited by my beliefs.*

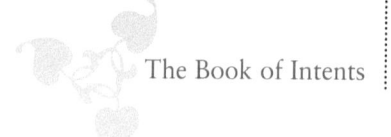

enthusiastic

# intent to be enthusiastic

*I am enthusiastic about my life experience.*

*I am filled with deep passion for life.*

*I feel excitement that is gushing and genuine.*

*It is my intent to smile for reasons and no reasons.*

enthusiastic

*I do only that which makes me completely excited and enthused.*

*I inspire with my own enthusiasm.*

*My enthusiasm knows no limit.*

abundant

# *intent to be abundant*

*I am abundant.*

*I am abundant in consciousness and love the journey of life.*

*I am full and over flowing with all the amazing goodness and luxury that exists.*

*It is my intent to be rich, welcome avalanches of large sums of money, prosperity,*

Abundant

flow of increasing income
from all directions.

I spend my abundance with
wisdom.

I flaunt my inner abundant
self, as it feels good.

It is my intent to invite love,
grace and freedom that
wealth brings, in its essence.

focus

# intent to focus

*I focus.*

*I focus on that which is good.*

*I train my thoughts to think, feel and know the power of focusing.*

*I breathe with such focus that I bring into my consciousness the true understanding and clarity of being here.*

*I focus to energize myself.*

focus

*I allow focus to happen gently and calmly.*

*I milk the good feeling moments in a way that they bring me to focus.*

Calm and
Composed

# intent to be calm and composed

I am calm and composed.

It is my intent to constantly affirm that, 'all this stuff does not move me'.

I welcome a strong sense of presence, freshness and awakened feeling within me towards life everyday.

Calm and
Composed

*I place my peace of mind as priority at every juncture and therefore feel the calmness as the external unfolds.*

*I allow the intuitive decision- letting it flow as I keep calm.*

*It is my intent to allow the best.*

*I float in calm and composed waters.*

Suspend
and
release

# *intent to suspend and release*

It is my intent to suspend and release.

I let go of all forms of judgment towards self and others.

I use my emotions to create good feelings and blessings for people and situations.

Suspend

and

release

*I let people be who they are.*

*I praise myself internally in such rewarding ways that there is no space for anything less.*

*I praise and create space for others to realize their own potential in time.*

*It is my intent to let love, inspiration, smiles, laughter, joy and ease be the backbone of my life.*

Connect

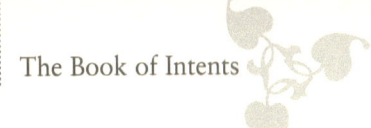

# *intent to connect*

I connect.

It is my intent to rendezvous with those who are loving life.

I release all insecurities and truly connect from a sense of goodness.

I am surrounded by powerful people who understand the significance of positive aspects.

Connect

*I live like a king and connect with those who enhance and enrich my experience.*

*I focus only on that which makes me feel good and tune out all else.*

*I engage with people from a genuine space of being able to see them as powerful creators, I value them, even though they may consciously not know who they are yet.*

# intent to stand in grace and be guiltless

It is my intent to stand in grace and therefore be guiltless in all moments.

I switch to grace instantly as that is my essence.

I am like the sea, wide open; majestic and royal.

I talk to every bit of me and that itself is a fascinating journey.

I *value my decisions and understand that nothing is really right or wrong, it is merely a choice, a path, a way.*

It is *my intent to enjoy the breeze that life is.*

I *acknowledge my feelings and remain in awareness of them.*

Inspired
action

# intent to relax and enjoy inspired action

I relax and enjoy inspired action.

It is my intent to meet the energy that creates worlds.

I train my thoughts to my good, to my happiness, to my invincibility, to my advantage.

Inspired
action

*I integrate with nature in a way that feels effortless.*

*I receive without conditions.*

*It is my intent to be successful and so satisfied with inspired action that, that's all I do for the rest of my life.*

*I welcome the Universe and invite it to meet me, match my vibration with abundant effortless ease.*

Acknowledge

# intent to acknowledge

I acknowledge all the love and care that the Universe has for me.

It is my intent to acknowledge ways in which the universe backs me up.

I paint my world colourful with fulfillment, wonderful dreams, growth, riches and all that truly belongs to me by Divine right.

Acknowledge

I accept all the amazing resources that life has already arranged for me.

I acknowledge how the universe supports my every move.

I acknowledge and receive all with love.

I appreciate my well-being, good health and success.

respect

# *intent to respect*

*It is my intent to respect.*

*I respect my feelings and emotions.*

*I inherit the truth of who I am in a way that feels settled.*

*I respect where I am and what I do.*

*It is my intent to recognize my truth.*

respect

*I respect my relationship
with God and see that respect
reflect in all my relationships.*

*I respect the essence of me.*

Visible

# intent to be visible

*I am visible like a winner.*

*I am convinced that the bestest things, situations, people are lining up for me.*

*It is my intent to be visible to self as a beautiful, forgiven, happy soul who is full of life.*

*I allow the universe to bring to me in complete sync and harmony every powerful,*

Visible

loving and strong resource in
time.

I allow myself to be visible in
all my glory.

I am comfortable being
visible.

I am created for a purpose
and that makes itself visible
to me.

The well being that I am
seeking, is seeking me and it
is my intent  that we meet in
grace.

Inherit my
kingdom

# intent to proudly inherit my kingdom

*I proudly inherit my kingdom.*

*I am one with the all flowing, awesome, abundance that life is.*

*I am in agreement with my decisions, I focus on that which feels good, stand still in the midst of it and enjoy the journey.*

Inherit my
kingdom

It is my intent to be so flowing and yet so still, to be so still and yet flow.

I expand my consciousness to richness, luxury, abundance and growth.

As I have the inner strength to be comfortable in groups, I open up to a wider audience.

It is my intent to see and be in my Paradise everyday.

# Serve and share

# intent to serve and share

I serve and share on a constant basis.

I am genuinely happy for the good of others.

I welcome platforms and ways where sharing is so easy, so comfortable, so graceful.

As I envision abundance for all, I truly enrich my own life experience.

# Serve and share

It is my intent to teach by example.

I share and serve from a space of seeing all of life worthy, deserving and prosperous.

I soar through life with well-being, brilliant health and leverage.

I apply myself effortlessly in the direction of my ever increasing pure power.

recognise

# intent to recognise myself as more than the person in this body

It is my intent to recognize myself as more than the person in this body.

I communicate easily with the broader, wiser part of me.

recognise

I expand that sweet spot inside me to finer dimensions of more good feelings.

I acknowledge the supreme consciousness within me.

It is my intent to bring in clarity and conviction into my life.

Every morning, I talk myself into appreciating this planet.

I smile my way into the mornings, afternoons, evenings and nights.

# intent to be strong

I am strong.

It is my intent to access this strength at all times.

The strength within me grows because I persist.

I feel my strength in my choices.

My inner strength is indestructible.

My strength is not limited by muscle, flesh and ego.

I smile in the face of resistance because I am strong.

I draw strength from being authentic.

Special

# Because you are special

*The sun shines and wishes you,*
*"Good-morning Brightness."*

*The stars sparkle and encourage you,*
*"Shine Away."*

*The moon descends and*
*acknowledges, "You Beautiful You."*

*The elements of spirit, earth, water,*
*air and fire join in complete unison*
*and balance to new levels of highness.*

*Life says, "You are doing so well."*

You can Contact the Author on the Below Platforms:

**e-mail:** healyourlife@rediffmail.com

**twitter:** shilpijchawla |

**Instagram:** Shilps_